Phonics Friends

Celine and Cedric
Go to the Circus
The Sound of Soft C

The
**Child's
World**

By Cecilia Minden and Joanne Meier

The Child's World

Published in the United States of America
by The Child's World®
PO Box 326
Chanhassen, MN 55317-0326
800-599-READ
www.childsworld.com

The Child's World®: Mary Berendes, Publishing Director

Editorial Directions, Inc.: E. Russell Primm, Editorial
Director and Project Editor; Katie Marsico, Associate
Editor; Judith Shiffer, Associate Editor and School Media
Specialist; Linda S. Koutris, Photo Researcher and
Selector

The Design Lab: Kathleen Petelinsek, Design and Page
Production

Photographs ©: Corbis/Michael S. Yamashita: 18; Getty
Images/digitalvision: 6; Getty Images/The Image Bank/
Darryl Estrine: 16; Getty Images/Photodisc Blue: 8;
Getty Images/Photodisc Green/Randy Allbritton: 10;
Getty Images/Photodisc Green/John A. Rizzo: 12; Getty
Images/Taxi/Suzanne Murphy: 14; Photo Edit, Inc./
Myrleen Ferguson Cate: cover, 4, 20.

Library of Congress Cataloging-in-Publication Data
Minden, Cecilia.
  Celine and Cedric go to the circus : the sound of soft C
/ by Cecilia Minden and Joanne Meier.
    p. cm. — (Phonics friends)
  Summary: Simple text featuring the sound of the soft
"c" describes two friends' trip to the circus.
  ISBN 1-59296-291-2 (library bound : alk. paper) [1.
English language—Phonetics. 2. Reading.] I. Meier,
Joanne D. II. Title. III. Series.
  PZ7.M6539Ce 2004
  [E]—dc22   2004003533

Note to parents and educators:

The Child's World® has created Phonics Friends with the goal of exposing children to engaging stories and pictures that assist in phonics development. The books in the series will help children learn the relationships between the letters of written language and the individual sounds of spoken language. This contact helps children learn to use these relationships to read and write words.

The books in this series follow a similar format. An introductory page, to be read by an adult, introduces the child to the phonics feature, or sound, that will be highlighted in the book. Read this page to the child, stressing the phonic feature. Help the student learn how to form the sound with her mouth. The Phonics Friends story and engaging photographs follow the introduction. At the end of the story, word lists categorize the feature words into their phonic element. Additional information on using these lists is on The Child's World® Web site listed at the top of this page.

Each book in this series has been carefully written to meet specific readability requirements. Close attention has been paid to elements such as word count, sentence length, and vocabulary. Readability formulas measure the ease with which the text can be read and understood. Each Phonics Friends book has been analyzed using the Spache readability formula. For more information on this formula, as well as the levels for each of the books in this series please visit The Child's World® Web site.

Reading research suggests that systematic phonics instruction can greatly improve students' word recognition, spelling, and comprehension skills. The Phonics Friends series assists in the teaching of phonics by providing students with important opportunities to apply their knowledge of phonics as they read words, sentences, and text.

The letter *c* makes two sounds.

The hard sound of *c* sounds like *c* as in:

>   *cap* and *coat.*

The soft sound of *c* sounds like *c* as in:

>   *celery* and *centipede.*

In this book, you will read words that
have the soft *c* sound as in:

>   *circus, city, cents,* and *circle.*

Celine and Cedric are excited.

They are going to the circus.

The circus is in the city.

A bus will take them to the city.

They wait and wait.

Here comes the bus.

It is ten cents to ride the bus.

The bus ride is fun!

Soon they are at the circus.

Cindy the clown is in the center ring. She makes Celine and Cedric laugh!

Here come the tigers.

They run fast around the circle.

Look at the monkey.

He is riding a bicycle.

Are you having fun?

We are certain we are!

Fun Facts

Early bicycles were called by several different names, including walking machines, bone shakers, and hobby horses. In the late 1800s, bicycle races became popular in the United States. Some of these races involved riders traveling nonstop for six days at a time! The winner was whomever could travel the farthest during this period.

Mumbai, India, is the largest individual city in the world and has more than 12 million residents. New York City is the largest individual city within the United States and has more than 8 million people. Scientists believe the first ancient cities appeared about 5,500 years ago.

Activity

A Bicycle Trip with Your Family

If you like bike riding, plan a bicycle trip with your family. Pick an area that has several good bike trails. Discuss what equipment you will need. Pack plenty of bottled water, sunscreen lotion, a healthy snack, and helmets. Take breaks every so often so you don't get too tired. Also, remember to be safe and to look out for other riders who share the trail with you.

To Learn More

Books
About Bicycles
Gibbons, Gail. *Bicycle Book*. New York: Holiday House, 1995.
Oxlade, Chris. *Bicycles*. Chicago: Heinemann Library, 2001.

About Circuses
Clements, Andrew, and Sue Truesdell (illustrator). *Circus Family Dog.*
  New York: Clarion Books, 2000.
Falconer, Ian. *Olivia Saves the Circus.* New York: Atheneum Books for
  Young Readers, 2001.

About Cities
Garland, Michael. *Christmas City*. New York: Dutton Children's Books, 2002.
Johnson, Stephen. *Alphabet City*. New York: Viking, 1995.

Web Sites
Visit our home page for lots of links about the Sound of Soft C:

http://www.childsworld.com/links.html

Note to Parents, Teachers, and Librarians: We routinely check our Web links to make
sure they're safe, active sites—so encourage your readers to check them out!

Soft C
Feature Words

Proper Names
Cedric
Celine
Cindy

Feature Words in
Initial Position
cent
center
certain
circle
circus
city

Feature Words in
Medial Position
bicycle
excited

About the Authors

Cecilia Minden, PhD, directs the Language and Literacy Program at the Harvard Graduate School of Education. She is a reading specialist with classroom and administrative experience in grades K–12. She earned her PhD in reading education from the University of Virginia. Cecilia and her husband Dave Cupp enjoy sharing their love of reading with their granddaughter Chelsea.

Joanne Meier, PhD, has worked as an elementary school teacher and university professor. She earned her BA in early childhood education from the University of South Carolina, and her MEd and PhD in education from the University of Virginia. She currently works as a literacy consultant for schools and private organizations. Joanne Meier lives with her husband Eric, and spends most of her time chasing her two daughters, Kella and Erin, and her two cats, Sam and Gilly, in Charlottesville, Virginia.